lidija šimkutė – wind sheen / 煌めく風

LIDIJA ŠIMKUTĖ
リジア・シュムクーテ

VĖJO ŽVILGESYS
WIND SHEEN
煌めく風

Translated into Japanese by Kōichi Yakushigawa

薬師川虹一／訳

Lidija Šimkutė's poems, many of them intimate miniatures, are original and expressive with a philosophical - spiritual tendency.

The author, subtly and precisely creates an original "metaphysical landscape" with unexpected connections.

Having a sound knowledge of both languages allows the author free reign to express herself in both languages, "intermixing" the original with the translation.

Antanas A. Jonynas

リジア・シュムクーテの詩は、極身近な世界に見えるが、実はとても独特な世界で、含蓄に富んだ哲学的で霊的な性質を持っている。

詩人は独創的な「形而上的風景」を予想もつかぬ組み合わせで微妙かつ正確に創り上げている。

詩人は二つの国語について健全な知識を持っているので、二つの言葉を自由に操り彼女自身を二つの言葉を縒り合わせて表現できるのだ。

アンタナス・A・ジョイナス

Antanas A. Jonynas（1953 b.）リトアニアの詩人、翻訳家。2011年に詩集 "The Rooms" を出す。内向的詩人であり、記憶の世界を描く。優れた翻訳家。

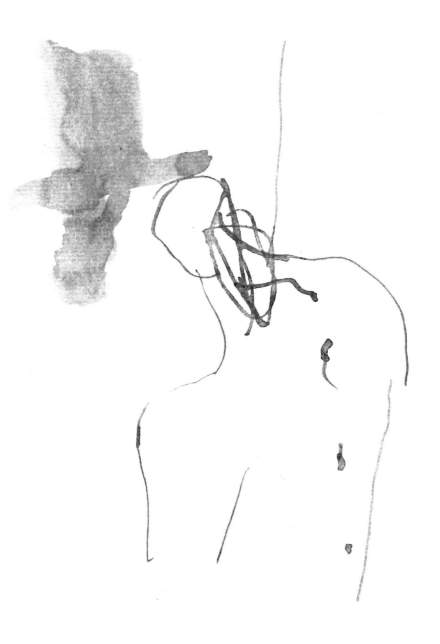

we have woken the birds
now they are feeding us

                    Christian Loidl

我らが鳥達を覚醒させたのだが
今じゃ彼らが我らを養っている

　　　クリスチャン・ロイドル

Christian Loidl（1957 – 2001）オーストリアの詩人。
イカロスのような生涯だった、と言われる。彼の言葉に「凝
視するに値するものは、凝視し得ないものだ」というのがある。

OCEAN HUM
大洋の囁き

The smell of the sea comes from somewhere
but I'm sure I can go further than the sea

Shuntaro Tanikawa

どこからか海の香りがやってくる
だけど絶対海を越えて行くぞ

谷川 俊太郎

谷川俊太郎詩集『はだか』の「とおく」より

SHEETS OF RAIN

cover my world

silver birds glint
through light

a ripple in my white cloth

the stillness of sea-shell
washes out into sand

海のシーツが

私の世界を覆う

銀色の鳥が
光を通して煌めく

私の白いシーツのさざ波が

貝の静寂を
砂の中へ洗い流す

PASSING CLOUDS

water the sea
in whispers
of forgotten rain

my shadow stretches
across grey drift

mounting the slopes
    of waves
        falling

去りゆく雲が

忘れられた雨の
囁きで
海をうるおしている

私の影は伸びる
灰色の波を越え

崩れ落ちる
　　　　波の坂を
　　　　　　　越えて

I EMERGE

as a seal

play like a dolphin
glide with the sharks
dive as a sea-lion

whale for the night

a sunfish at dawn

私は現れる

アザラシとなって

イルカのように戯れ
サメと共に滑り
トドのように潜る

夜はクジラ

朝はマンボウ

CLOSE MY LIPS

with your voice
seagull of
velvet eyes

let us become sky

    breathing

        sun

ビロードの目を持つ

カモメよ
あなたの声で
私の唇を塞いでおくれ

共に大空となって

　　　吸い込もうよ

　　　　　　太陽を

I STEP INTO THE SEA

*scatter pomegranate
waves to the wind*

*salt skin flowers
into disappearance*

DROWNING

the ocean

*we throw dice
in pebble madness*

私は海に踏み込み

風に向かって
ザクロの波をまき散らそう

潮焼けた肌は
消滅へと花開く

溺れ行く

滄海

私達は狂気の小石となって
ダイスを投げる

BEFORE THE FINAL DREAM

I give back the bread
to earth and sea

who will assemble the pieces
into a loaf of sun

夢の果てる前に

私はパンを返そう
大地と海に

パンくずは集まって
ひと山の太陽になるだろう

THE DRUM OF PINES

over ocean hum

awakens the sun

the albatross flight

sea reveals its rocks

clouds watch
the juniper blaze

松林のドラムが

大洋のつぶやきを超えて

太陽を目覚ます

アルバトロスの飛翔

海はその暗礁を剥き出し

雲はエニシダの
炎上を見詰める

YOUNG MEN

with faces like flames
sprawl the seaside
with empty bottles

girls hoist their wet
robes to the moon

serene as sea-weed clouds

the wave whale yawns
and falls asleep in the sand

starfish shine through
                the stones

若者たちは

顔を火照らせ
海辺に
空き瓶を撒き散らす

娘たちは濡れた水着を
月に向かって掲げる

海草の雲の如く長閑

浪のクジラはあくびをし
砂の中に眠り込み

ヒトデは小石の中で
　　　　　　　煌めいている

THE SEA WAILS

in early winter

a flap of injured wings
stirs the silver white lining

wind ripples
awaken the air
and peel away the skin
*   from sky*

海が泣くのは

冬の始まる頃

傷ついた羽根の羽ばたきが
白銀の水平線をかき乱す

風の細波が
大気を目覚まし
空の薄肌を
　　　剥きはがす

THE OLD MAN

*sits with his back
against the tomb
mending his nets*

*his wife
knits green sea
curtains in the shade*

*walking among the
stones I unravel
            sleep*

老人は

墓石に
凭れて
網を繕う

木陰の老妻は
緑の海で
カーテンを編む

私は小石の間を
歩きながら
　　　眠りをほどく

SHELL OF SEA

shell of wind

where flags of white
feathers fly

how the seagulls scythe
under sun and sky

I circle like smoke
from the ship of the dead

海の貝

風の貝

そこは白い羽根の
はためく処

煌めく陽光と空のもと
カモメたちの巧みな刈り取りの技

幽霊船から立ち昇る
煙のように私は舞う

BIRDS CROSS

his shadow and
die from height

far below
screams are reborn
in the froth of
the fanged sea

カモメは

影を切り裂いて
死の急降下

悲鳴は
牙をむく
波間に
復活する

ONE SEAGULL

*or was it a thought
that flickered by*

一羽のカモメ

それともきらりと
通り過ぎた想い

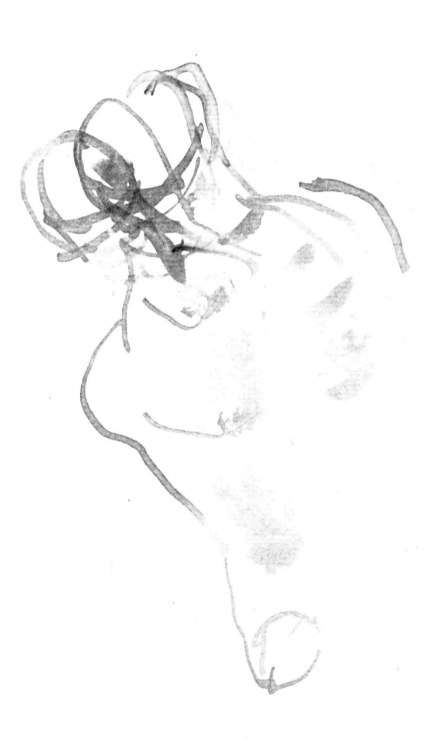

ECHO OF TREES
樹　霊

for echo is the soul of the voice
exciting itself in hollow places

Michael Ondaatje

木霊は声の霊だから
深みでは一層昂るの

マイケル・オンダーチェ

　　Michael Ondaatje(1943 −)スリランカ生まれのカナダの詩人。
　『イギリス人の患者』で1992年、英国のブッカー賞を受賞。

I RETURN

from where I came
abandoned and found again
under transparent sky

I walk by the river
that refuses to cry

it stretches across
time-wasted landscape
where blades split the dawn

I wade in dew grass
let the wind drum
my barefoot existence

hands open clench

I walk on riverbed stones
pick up the pebbles

throw them into a stream

私は戻る

私の来たところから
諦めては取り戻し
空はどこまでも透明

私は川岸を歩くが
川は決して泣かない

老衰した風景を越えて
川は流れ
やがて刃が曙の空を切り裂く

露の草原を渉ると
私の素足の実感を
風が轟かせる

両掌は拳を開き

私は石の川床を歩く
小石を拾い

流れの中に投げ込む

MY MOTHER

sits
    and watches
the red river gums in the creek
the daily strollers with their dogs
the roses and shrubs
she planted years ago

she nods

the white corellas screech
the kookaburras laugh

she hears

the nightingale
in her village

母は

  座って
    見詰めている
溝川をねっとりと流れる赤い川
犬を連れて毎日散歩する人達
薔薇や花の茂みは
母が何年か前に植えたもの

母が頷く

白いオウムの金切り声
カワセミの笑い声

母が聞いているのは

村で歌う
鶯の声

THE HAZED MARKET PLACE

entwines
voices tumbling
from hanging gardens

a serpent-tailed horse
flies into the night fog

広場には霞がかかり

空中庭園から
転げ落ちる嬌声と
絡み合っている

蛇のように尻尾を靡かせた馬が
霧の夜空へと飛び込んでゆく

THE CITY'S EYES

change color and form

washed sky
dresses bare roofs

the day swallows the dream

都会の目は

色も形も変える

澄みきった青空が
裸の屋根の身繕いをする

昼は夢を呑みこむ

THE UŽUPIS*

walls of Vilnius whisper

around corners
spider webs
wait in suspense

roof drains flower

a dream born from hunger

* ex-slums of the Lithuanian capital

ウズピス*は

ヴィリニュスの風説の壁

街角を曲がれば
蜘蛛の巣が
不安げに待ちうける

屋根の花は枯れ

一つの夢が飢えから生まれる

* ウズピス UŽUPIS：リトアニアの首都の昔のスラム

WHEN BONES IN THE DARK

read fingerprints

the knife in water
swallowed by night
re-enters the day

a turn of events
slices sinister hours
dispersing them
into phosphorescent weeks

the cuts of palms
hold their own stories

骨が闇の中で

指紋の意味を読み解く時

水中のナイフが
夜に呑みこまれ
昼に再生する

事件の展開が
不安な時を切りきざみ
微かに光る
日々の中へ消散させる

掌の切れ端にも
それぞれの物語がある

A DAY VEILED

in rain

*when shadows of
things tremble*

*face echoes face
wall become mirrors*

一日が

雨の中で曇るとき

様々な影が
震えだす

顔が顔に応え
壁が鏡となる

MY FATHER

emerged from the coffin

and told me it could be
mine in the year to come

I'm bored

he said

below all is water
and above hungry dust

he tilted his head

by the light of his match

I saw neither myself
                nor another

私の父が

棺桶から出てきて

私に言った何れはお前も
こうなるだろう

項垂れる私

彼は言う

下界は全て水
天界は飢えた塵芥

彼はうなだれ

燐寸の火をともすが

その光で私には私自身の
　　　　　　姿さえ見えない

THE NIGHT

with gleaming teeth

bit the moon
in the plum-skin sky

STARLIGHT

bites through the sky

figs hang heavy with sleep

夜が

きらりと光る歯で

李の皮のような空に浮かぶ
月を嚙んだ

星影が

空を突き抜けて

眠たげにだらりと垂れたイチジクを嚙む

TO MELT OR TO FREEZE

was etched into stone

to break or to bend
echoed through trees

to flow or to burn
churned in the head

the circle of the living
the tree of the dead

溶けるためか固まるためか
石に刻まれるのは

折れるためかやり過ごすためか
木立の中で木霊するのは

溢れ出るためか噴出するためか
脳髄の中で沸騰するのは

生者の円環よ
死者の樹よ

COAL ISLAND

Water
shapes a shadow

early black becomes
the deep of tree

石炭の島

海は
陰となり

夜明け前の黒い陰は
深い森となる

THE GUMS

are shedding their bark

pollen scatters its haze
on railway-sleeper table

morning-glory entwines
trellis and fence

listens to echo of trees

hydrangeas and agapanthus
stand in wondering light

I shed my skin

ユーカリが

樹皮を脱ぎ

花粉の霞が
枕木の上に広がる

曙の光が
格子戸や垣根に絡み

木立の木霊に耳を傾ける

訝(いぶか)しげな光の中に立つ
アジサイとクンシラン

私は脱皮する

I DIMINISH

*into a spray of flowers
under river mist*

私は小さくなって

川霧に包まれた
花穂となる

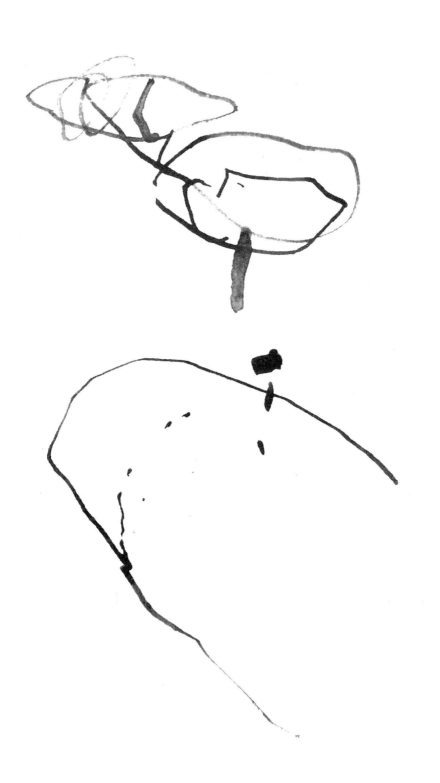

SUN DOORS
太陽の扉

Fire utters not a word

Gennadji Aigji

火は一言も喋らない

ゲンナジイ・アイギ

Gennadji Aigji（1934 – 2006）チュヴァシの詩人。
リジアさんはリトアニアでの詩祭で会ったと言う。

CHANCE MEETING

of eyes
hinge on sun doors

breathless windows
slow tumble of voices
          seeking

ふと出会った

目と目が
太陽の扉に固まる

息をのむ窓
声がゆっくり寝転び
　　　　　　求めている

I KNEW YOUR VOICE

before your name

paper soaks up
the remains of an instant

in colours
of ink
and blood

声で判ったよ

名前を聞く前に

紙が吸い上げるのは
一瞬の残像

インクと
　　　血の
　　　　色の

RED BREAD

blue wine

my love's silent hair

EYES IN THE WATER

wash away thought

the willow's bend
withdraws
in a no-motion dance

赤いパン

青いワイン

恋人のもの言わぬ髪の毛

水の中の目は

想いを洗い流す

枝垂れ柳が
動きを止めたダンスの形で
舞台を去る

STALKS OF ACHE

and ecstasy

we hold clouds
and feel the languid air
take the shape of wings

moss ripples whisper
and engrave pebbles

with passing river song

忍びよるのは

痛みと恍惚

曇天を抱え
物憂い風を感じながら
翼の形をとる

苔の細波が囁き
流れる川の歌を

小石に刻む

TIME FREEZES

I ponder all the night

shine my eyes

have gathered

and stroke the moon
flakes on your sleeve

時は凍り

私は夜通しものを想い

両目を光らせて

月のかけらを

集めては
君の袖に叩きつけてきた

THE GIFT

of slow passing time

holds night scent

let's stop time

and hold each other

贈り物は

ゆっくり進む時間

夜の香りを抱えている

時間を止めよう

抱き合おう

THE SMILE

wider than a cloud
under the Blue Tower
from a grey Stockholm sky

is it a Springbird
    or a Strindberg

        wanting to fly

頬笑みは

雲よりも広く
ブルータワーの下
灰色のストックホルムの空から

スプリングバードかな
　　　ストリンドバーグかな

　　　　　飛びたがっているのは

Johan August Strindberg（ヨハン・アウグスト・ストリンドベリ）
（1849 - 1912）スウェーデンの劇作家。

A HEAD FULL OF SPACE

forgets the hours

tea stirs in my cup

your face
between my thoughts

空っぽの頭は

時間を忘れ

お茶はコップの中で渦を巻く

君の顔は
いろんな想いの中に

WHEN EYES

follow clouds
behind
the white ceiling

plaster and skin
memory
and pain

become one
white shadow

眼が雲の

後を追う時
白い天井の
向こうでは

シックイとスキン
記憶と
苦痛が

一つになって
白い影となる

PETUNIAS

your eyes dissolve
into clusters
            of velvet

IN MY ABSENCE

I'll fill the pages
of your books

with ocean fragrance

ペチュニア

君の眸は溶けて
ベルベットの
　　　　　毯となる

姿をかくして

私は貴方の
本の頁を

海の香りで満たしておこう

YOU SWEEP

*the dust
from my mind*

*you bite through
the skin of my sleep*

*bird shadows gather
on my tongue*

*and sing what
memory can't keep*

あなたは掃き出す

私の胸から
余計なものを

眠りの薄皮ごしに
そっと噛む

鳥の影が
舌の上に集まり

記憶に残らない
歌を歌う

NOW THAT WE ARE PARTING

rain has returned

*I want to be nothing only the
fragrance of some scattered
rose and pass like smoke*

now that we are parting

*the music will fall and settle
in the pages of your books
and wait to be opened*

now that we are parting

*my eyes follow invisible
birds across the ceiling*

hands become wind

*and earth turns faster
than a night ago*

*I leave a white cloud
in your hands*

now that we are parting

*I will dress in rain and
watch the warmth behind
some distant window slowly*

take on your name

今私達は別れるのだ
また降りだした

私は何にもなりたくない
唯散ったバラの香りだけ
そして煙のように去りたい

今私達は別れるのだ

あなたの想い出の頁の中に
この時の調べは落ち着き
開かれるときを待つ

今私達は別れるのだ

私の目は空を渡る
見えない鳥を追っている

両掌は風となり

地球は昨夜より
早く回転し

私は貴方の両掌の中に
白い雲を残していく

今私達は別れるのだ

私は雨をまとい
何処か遠い窓の向こうの
温もりを見詰めて

あなたの名前をそっと抱える

GREENFIELD

at dusk

our mingled breath
returns to the landscape

緑の野原は

夕暮れの中

二人の吐息が縺れて
風景に戻る

WIND SHEEN
煌めく風

I have made a room in the wind

Ken Smith

私は風の中に部屋を造った

ケン・スミス

Kenneth John Smith（1938 - 2003）リーズ（Leeds）から新声としてデビュー。最後の詩集『流されて』は2002年出版。

THE FIRST NOTE

of cicadas

wakes in tree tops
against the hiss of wind

dusk spreads
silver sheen
along the shore

wind turns from
salt into melon

蝉の

初音が

梢で目覚め
風の悲鳴に逆らう

夕暮れが
銀色のきらめきを
岸辺に広げ

風は塩から
メロンに変わる

GULLS SHRIEK

above sun
bitten pavement

lump sugar houses
cluster the razor
black hillside

fig tree dotted
pastures sink into
oleander sleep

amidst dragon-fly darts
and shadows shifting

the fisherboy's
clarinet drawl
        unrolls
            the sea

かもめが鳴く

太陽の彼方
噛みつかれた鋪道

角砂糖の家なみ
剃刀の群れ
黒ずむ丘

点在するイチジク
牧場は沈む
夾竹桃の眠りの中へ

中空を翔ぶ蜻蛉
影がゆれる

若い漁師の
クラリネットが
　　　　　ゆっくりと
　　　　　　　海にほどける

WATERMELON SUN

drops into mist

a white cat
weaves through
wooden tables and chairs

from some sullen dome
with no minaret
a far away call
arches in with
diluted song

西瓜の太陽が

靄の中に落ちる

白い猫が
木造のテーブルと椅子の間を
縫って駆け抜ける

ミナレットの無い
陰気なドームから
遠い呼び声が
気の抜けた歌声とともに
弧を描いて来る

SEA-BIRDS SCREECH

in melon scented air

sun-beaten sails
spread the sea
to the purple agate portal
curved lips

the horizon recedes and
surrenders to sails

wave waves to wave

海鳥たちが甲高く鳴く

メロンの香りが漂う

日焼けした帆が
海風を孕み
紫瑪瑙(めのう)の港は
唇を開く

水平線は退き
白帆は勝ち誇る

波は波と頷きあう

WIND TORN MINARET

curved against heat
gathers dust

needle-brushing
the cicadas silence

風に引き裂かれたミナレットは

熱風に身をのけぞらせ
砂埃にまみれる

針のブラシに
蝉は沈黙する

CRACKS OF LIGHT

between shutters

bleached sun winds its way
from nowhere

wind sheen daggers a faded
palm out of its sleep

sea sheet unfolds over rocks

sea gulls cry the windows out

シャッターの隙間に

光が弾ける

漂白された太陽が
どこからか忍び込む

煌めく風の短剣が
疲れ果てた棕櫚の葉を目覚ませる

海のシーツが岩に広がり

カモメたちの叫び声が風を追い払う

WHITE COLUMNS

in cobalt heat
steam away thought

bouzouki quivers
in half-light

lean cats loiter
under vines and
bougainvillaea

with no sea-gulls in sight
the sea stops breathing

白い柱が

コバルト色の熱気の中で
想いを蒸気で吹き飛ばす

ブズーキが薄明の中に
トレモロを流し

痩せ猫が
葡萄棚とブーゲンビリアの
下をうろつく

カモメたちの姿は無く
海は息をのんでいる

　　　ブズーキ　bouzouki：マンドリンに似たギリシャの弦楽器

SEA-COLOURED EYES

colour
the cities we see

in the mirror of thirst
the Baltic green deepens

海色の眸が

眼の前の街並みを
染める

干からびた鏡の中で
バルト海の緑が深まる

THE BLUE WOOL

hung entangled
in her hands

she followed the thread
to its end

she buried her hands
in the sand

her eyes entered clouds
her hair spread
dune grass

with lips of coral
she touched blue sand

and lost her fingers
*   to the sky*

青色の毛糸が

彼女の両手のなかで
縺れて垂れている

彼女は糸を手繰り
端を引き寄せる

彼女は両手を
砂に埋め

彼女の両の眼は
雲に埋もれ髪は
砂丘の草に広がる

サンゴの唇で
青い砂に口づけする

彼女の指は
　　　　空に消える

A GRAIN OF WIND

*returns from
the ink stained sky*

*bones read before time
the breath of the living*

*the body speech
of the dead*

風が一粒

インクの滲んだ空から
吹き戻る

遺骨は嘗ての
生者の吐息を読み

遺骸は死者のことを
語る

SEA GRASS

among waves
wears out stone

I erode my shadow
in passing

WIND

shapes
thought

to the other world I call
to the other world I yield

海の草は

波間に漂い
石をすり減らす

私は通りすがりに
自分の影を消している

風は

想いを
象り

私はあの世に呼びかけ
あの世に身を任す

PINES

dressed
in salt-green

sway on the
edge of a cliff

each needle
threads into song

松の木が

利休鼠の
ドレスをまとい

崖の縁で
揺れると

針がそれぞれ
調べを紡ぎ出す

Lidija Šimkutė was born in a small village in Samogitia, Lithuania. After WWII spent her early childhood in displaced persons camps in Germany; arrived in Australia 1949. Extended her studies by correspondence in Lithuanian language, folklore and literature (1973-78) through the Lithuanian Language Institute, Chicago, USA and went to Vilnius University, Lithuania in 1977 & 1987 for summer language courses. Worked professionally as a dietitian in Perth, (W.A.) and Adelaide S.A.) . After retiring divides her time between the two countries and is widely travelled.

Šimkutė writes in Lithuanian and English: published in literary journals / anthologies in Australia, Lithuania and elsewhere incl. *The World Poetry Almanac* (2008, 2010) and the *Turnrow Anthology of Contemporary Australian Poetry 2013* (USA). Her poetry has been translated into sixteen languages (*Arabic, Bulgarian, Esperanto, Estonian, German, Gaelic, Georgian, Italian, Japanese, Latvian, Macedonian, Polish, Russian, Slovenian, Spanish, Ukrainian*). She has translated Australian and other poetry ,including Japanese*/ prose into Lithuanian and Lithuanian poetry into English. Read her work in various countries and at International Poetry Festivals.

Lithuanian, Ukrainian and Australian choreographers have used her poetry in modern dance/theatrical poetry performances with readings in Australia, (*WWW-Lake George, Weerewa Festival*, 2002, and *Dreaming the Deep* in European countries, Ukraine *"The Chair"* in *Les Kurbos Theatre*, Lviv, 2001 as well as in Lithuania (*Spaces of Silence* productions in Vilnius, Kaunas and Klaipeda theatres, 2005).

Lithuanian, Australian and British composers have used Šimkutė's poetry in their compositions, performed by various ensembles in Lithuania, European countries, England and Australia. Lidija read before Margery Smith's compositions 1) *White Shadows* was premiered at *The Sydney Opera House - Utzon recital hall by Hourglass ensemble*, and 2) *Ocean Hum* (extended) at *The Flute Tree studio by Grevillea ensemble in Oct. 2015*. Šimkutė has received literary grants from Australian, South Australian and Australian Lithuanian Foundation councils.

リジア・シュムクーテはリトアニアのサモギチアに在る小さな村に生まれた。第二次世界大戦後ドイツの難民キャンプで幼少期を過ごし、1949にオーストラリアに移住した。1973–78シカゴのリトアニア言語学院でリトアニアの言語、民話、文学を学び、1977と1987にはリトアニアのヴィルニュス大学夏季言語コースで学んだ。のち西オーストラリアのパースや南オーストラリのアデレイドで栄養士の教授として働いた。退職後リトアニア・オーストラリア両国をまたいで仕事をし、多くの国で活動している。

シュムクーテはリトアニア語と英語とを使って仕事をし、作品は様々な国の多くの文芸誌やアンソロジー、例えば、*The World Poetry Almanac*(2008–2010),*Turnrow Anthology of Contemporary Australian Poetry 2013*等でも発表されている。彼女の詩は16ヵ国語に翻訳されている。彼女はオーストラリア語その他日本語を含む国語の詩や散文をリトアニア語に、リトアニア語の詩を英語に翻訳し、また自作の詩を様々な国や国際詩祭で朗読している。また様々なミュージシャンと共に2ヵ国語による5巻のCDを発表している。
リトアニア、ウクライナ、オーストリア、及びオーストラリアの振り付け師たちが彼女の詩を現代ダンス、演劇詩の公演などに用いている。

リトアニア、オーストラリア、イギリスの作曲家たちも彼女の詩を作品の中に使用しているし、リトアニア、ポーランド、ロシア、イギリス、オーストラリアなどでアンサンブルとして上演されている。その中には、マージェリー・スミスの*White Shadows*も含まれている。

Poetry publications in Lithuanian: *The Second Longing* 1978, *Anchors of Memory* 1982, **(USA)**; *Wind and Roots* 1991 **(Lithuania)**; **in English**: *The Sun Paints a Sash*, 2000 **(USA)**; **Bilingual:** *Tylos erdvės / Spaces of Silence* -(foreword David Malouf),1999; *Vėjo žvilgesys/ Wind Sheen*- (foreword Antanas A. Jonynas)- 2003); *Mintis ir uola / Thought and Rock*- (foreword JM Coetzee), 2008; *Kažkas pasakyta / Somehting is said*- (foreword Tomas Venclova), 2013; *Baltos vaivorykštės / White Rainbows*-(foreword Jan Owen, 2016) **(Lithuania)**; **Translations:**-*Weisse Schatten / White Shadows*- (translation & foreword Christian Loidl) - **Austria**, 2000; *Iš toli ir arti / Z bliska i z daleka*, (translation Sigitas Birgelis)- **Poland**, 2003; *Thought and Rock / 想いと磐 ,,* 2014; *Something is said / 何かが語られる* , 2016; *White Rainbows /* リジア・シュムクーテ Japan, 2018. Translation & afterwords by Kōichi Yakushigawa) .

Book Translation into Lithuanian: David Malouf –*An Imaginary Life*- Vilnius, 2002.

Other Book Publications
***Lietuviški Ex Libris   Lithuanian Bookplates*-** Australian Lithuanian Foundation,1980
***Contemporary Lithuanian Bookplates* -** Australian Lithuanian Foundation, 1989

CD Publications - Bilingual with musician, music or sound inserts
Klausykim vėjo / Listen to the Wind – Boris Kovareč ABC radio 2000/08
Tylos erdvės / Spaces of Silence - Hildegard von Bingen & Eric Satie, 2004
Vėjo žvilgesys / Wind Sheen - Gediminas Sederevičius, Japanese flute, 2006
Balti šešėliai / White Shadows - Saulius Šiaučiulis, piano, 2008
Mintis ir uola / Thought and Rock- Anita Hustas, double bass, 2014

Eglė, Queen of the Serpents - Lithuanian Folktale - A.Smolskus, reed-pipe
 - translated and told by Lidija Šimkutė
*Kōichi Yakushigawa:
 Literature & Art : (Spiral) - *Lithuania*, Nov.24, 2006
 Literature & Art: (the Fatal Moment) - *Lithuania*, July 23, 2010
 Šiaurės Atėnai: (Wastepaper basket) - *Lithuania*, Sept, 2014
 Literature & Art: (Sand Glass) – *Lithuania*, March, 2016
 Naujoji Romuva- (Conversations with Stone Buddha) three poems, No 1, 2018

リトアニア語による詩集：*The Second Longing* 1978, *Anchors of Memory* 1982, *Wind and Roots* 1991, 英語による詩集：*The Sun Paints a Sash*, 2000, 二カ国語による詩集：*Spaces of Silence* 1999, *Wind Sheen*, 2003, *Thought and Rock*, 2008, *Something is said*, 2013, *White Rainbows*, 2016

翻訳　英語・日本語：『想いと磐』2014,『何かが語られる』2016,『白い虹』2018,『煌めく風』2019 (to be)

 **Kōichi Yakushigawa** b. 1929 in Kyoto. Poet, translator (incl Phillip Larkin, Seamus Heaney & others, including Lidija Šimkutė's four poetry books,) photographer, professor emeritus. Previous editor of "Ravine" literary journal. On the Board of directors, Kansai Poetry Society. Taught English and literature at Doshisha University. Kyoto. Retired 2004. On the Board of Directors of International Byron Society. President emeritus of the Japanese Byron Society.

Awards: The Kyoto City Art and Culture Association Prize 1997, The Order of the Sacred Treasure, Gold Rays with Neck Ribbon 2010, Translator's Special Prize from Japan Translators Society 2014.

Books published:
Poems; "Cityscape with an old dog" and others
Poems & Photos; Talking with Stone Buddha" and others
Academic; "A Study on the British Romantic Poets and Their Social Background" "Reading the Seamus Heaney's World" and others.

薬師川 虹一
1929年京都に生まれる。詩人、随筆家、写真家、翻訳者（フィリップ・ラーキン、シェイマス・ヒーニー、テッド・ヒューズ・リジア・シュムクーテ等）、英文学者（イギリス・ロマン派詩人の研究）、同志社大学名誉教授、詩誌「RAVINE」前編集同人。日本バイロン協会名誉会長。国際バイロン協会前理事。

受賞歴：京都芸術文化協会賞
　　　　日本翻訳家協会特別賞、瑞宝中綬章

出版書：詩集『疲れた犬のいる風景』他
　　　　詩と写真集『石仏と語る』他
　　　　研究書『イギリスロマン派の研究』他

Translator's Postscript

Some of the poems by Lidija Šimkutė have already been translated by myself and introduced on the Website of the Kansai Poets' Association. However, I retranslated many of them for the publication of this book.

Her poems are articulate and direct reflections of her sensibility, avoiding any explanatory wordings. We should not look for grammatical sequences in her poems but rely on our own sensibility to read them. Accordingly, her poems are not easy to comprehend, and therefore, they are so attractive to us all.

When we read her poems, our sensibilities are always challenged. Therefore, translating her poems is no wonder the hardest ordeal; what is required is not a language skill but poetical sensibility. Translating her poems is not replacing the words, but re-creating poems which reflect her sensibility and breathing. Should I make a mistranslation, it would not because of my language ability but because of my poetical sense.

Translating her poems, I sometimes thought of the days when I translated late Seamus Heaney's poems. That was a difficult task, too, but the difficulty this time was different from the one in the past with Seamus Heaney. Heaney's poems and his world were very difficult to comprehend, but listening to his words, I could finally manage to complete my translation. On the other hand, Lidija Šimkutė's poems would not explain anything. Readers should try to find her ideas from the blank

訳者あとがき

　この詩集のうちのいくつかは、以前関西詩人協会のHPに翻訳して載せていただいたことがあるが、この度、新たに一冊の詩集全体の翻訳として訳しなおしたものが多い。彼女の詩は一切の説明をそぎ落とした、極めて直截な作品なので、文法的な言葉の繋がりはほとんど無視とまでは言わないが、極めて不明確な場合が多い。したがって、彼女の詩を読む時は、読者の感性が大きく作用することになる。
　彼女の詩を読むとき、読者は自らの感性を試されることになる。当然翻訳は、苦しい仕事になる。文字面だけを読むのではなく、書いている時の彼女の心、というか、息遣い、というようなものを感じていないと読めないことが多い。したがって、翻訳は、入学試験の英文和訳、のような作業ではなく、詩人と詩人の真剣勝負の様相を帯びざるを得ない。
　誤訳があるとすれば、辞書的・文法的な誤訳ではなく、訳者の感性の乏しさに依るものとなるだろう。彼女の詩集を翻訳するとき、私はいつもそう思っている。これは、昔仲間とともにシェイマス・ヒーニーの詩集を完訳していたときと全く質の異なる難しさなのだ。文字になる以前の彼女の想いを掴まねばならない。彼女の文字は何も語ってくれない。文字の間、行の間、スタンザの間、の空間に彼女の想いが潜んでいる。その空間を訳出しなければならない訳者の日本語力が試される。恐ろしい仕事なのだ。だから僕はこの仕事に取り憑かれているともいえるだろう。
　この詩集は、2003年に発行されたものである。今までに訳出してきた三冊の詩集の前の詩集となる。今、この詩集の前、2000年に出された詩集『白い影』の翻訳に取りかかっている。五冊の詩集を読めば、彼女の想いに少しは近づけるのではない

space between words and lines. The translator had to translate the blank space into his own language.

Think of some Japanese paintings. A blank, unpainted space is often considered as one of the most significant characteristics of Japanese paintings, which can hardly be seen in Western paintings. When I was translating her poems, I was thinking of this difference between Western art and Japanese art.

Having translated her poems for about 20 years, recently I do not find it so difficult to comprehend her poems. I have found that she is like a very delicate landscape painter. As an artist, she would not paint landscape exactly as it looks. She rejects all the despotism of the eyes. She looks at the landscape *within* her eyes, or she looks at the landscape *within* the landscape. Such images could be called "Inscape". She may be called a poet of "Inscape". (She may not care for this name, though ….)

Lastly, please permit me to introduce a poem – the one she wrote for me.

Lidija Šimkutė
for Kōichi Yakushigawa

YOUR BIRD FLIGHT
from Kyoto to Vilnius
brought Indian summer

だろうか、と思いながら訳している。

　近頃彼女の詩がとても判り易くなってきたように思う。つまり彼女はとても繊細な風景画家なのだ。勿論見たままの風景ではないことは言うまでもない。彼女の心の目を通して見える風景なのだ。以前シェイマス・ヒーニーの詩を訳していたとき、彼の詩集の表題に、SEEING THINGS というのがあった。「物を見る」と訳したのではなんともならない英語である。「物の本質を見る」とでも訳せばいいのだが、それではなんとなく納まりが悪いので、「物の奥を見る」としてみたことがある。リジアさんの場合もそんな感じではないだろうか。風景 landscape というのではなく、彼女の眼の奥に煌めいた風景 inscape という言葉を使った批評家がいたのを思い出す。

　その意味では彼女は inscape の風景画家だと言ってみたい。彼女がなんと言うかは判らないが……。

　拙い翻訳ではあるが、ほぼ二十歳の年の差がある彼女の詩をなんとか正しく受けとめたいと思いながら翻訳している。拙訳をご寛恕いただければ幸甚と言わねばなるまい。

　最後にいささか私ごとになりますが、リジアさんが私に詩を書いて送ってくれました。ここに加えて礼儀を尽くさせていただきます。

薬師川　虹一に
　　　　　リジア・シュムクーテ

あなたの小鳥が
京都からヴィリニュスへ
小春日和を運んできました

in the joy of meeting
we talked over tea
in black madonna's
      embrace
near The Gates of Dawn*

intermittent words
remain in my senses

fall into oblivion
      rise
        then descend
by the Druskininkai* lake

where Zen butterflies
      continue tracing
        our steps

*   Gates of Dawn house the black madonna
*   Lithuanian Autumn Poetry Festival resourt city
   where we met for the first time in 2014

November 11, 2018
Kōichi Yakushigawa

お会いできた嬉しさに
私たちはお茶を挟み
曙の門*に祀られる
　　　　黒い聖母に
抱かれて語り合いましたね

とぎれとぎれの言葉が今でも
私の五感の内に残っています

忘却の中に沈み
　　　　浮かび
　　　　　　また沈み
傍らにはドルスキニンカイ*の湖

そこでは禅僧のような
　　　　蝶が二匹戯れながら
　　　　　　私たちを追っています

*　　黒い聖母はそこの教会に祀られている。
*　　ドルスキニンカイはリトアニア国際詩祭が毎年開かれるところ。

2018年9月11日
乱雑な机に向かって
薬師川虹一記す

Contents

OCEAN HUM · 15
    SHEETS OF RAIN · 16
    PASSING CLOUDS · 18
    I EMERGE · 20
    CLOSE MY LIPS · 22
    I STEP INTO THE SEA · 24
    DROWNING · 24
    BEFORE THE FINAL DREAM · · · · · · · · · · · · · · 26
    THE DRUM OF PINES · 28
    YOUNG MEN · 30
    THE SEA WAILS · 32
    THE OLD MAN · 34
    SHELL OF SEA · 36
    BIRDS CROSS · 38
    ONE SEAGULL · 40

ECHO OF TREES · 45
    I RETURN · 46
    MY MOTHER · 48
    THE HAZED MARKET PLACE · · · · · · · · · · · · · · 50
    THE CITY'S EYES · 52
    THE UŽUPIS · 54
    WHEN BONES IN THE DARK · · · · · · · · · · · · · · 56
    A DAY VEILED · 58
    MY FATHER · 60
    THE NIGHT · 62
    STARLIGHT · 62
    TO MELT OR TO FREEZE · · · · · · · · · · · · · · · · · 64
    COAL ISLAND · 66
    THE GUMS · 68
    I DIMINISH · 70

目次

大洋の囁き ……………………………… 15
 海のシーツが ……………………… 17
 去りゆく雲が ……………………… 19
 私は現れる ………………………… 21
 ビロードの目を持つ ……………… 23
 私は海に踏み込み ………………… 25
 溺れ行く …………………………… 25
 夢の果てる前に …………………… 27
 松林のドラムが …………………… 29
 若者たちは ………………………… 31
 海が泣くのは ……………………… 33
 老人は ……………………………… 35
 海の貝 ……………………………… 37
 カモメは …………………………… 39
 一羽のカモメ ……………………… 41

樹　霊 …………………………………… 45
 私は戻る …………………………… 47
 母は ………………………………… 49
 広場には霞がかかり ……………… 51
 都会の目は ………………………… 53
 ウズピスは ………………………… 55
 骨が闇の中で ……………………… 57
 一日が ……………………………… 59
 私の父が …………………………… 61
 夜が ………………………………… 63
 星影が ……………………………… 63
 溶けるためか固まるためか ……… 65
 石炭の島 …………………………… 67
 ユーカリが ………………………… 69
 私は小さくなって ………………… 71

SUN DOORS · 75
- CHANCE MEETING · 76
- I KNEW YOUR VOICE · 78
- RED BREAD · 80
- EYES IN THE WATER · 80
- STALKS OF ACHE · 82
- TIME FREEZES · 84
- THE GIFT · 86
- THE SMILE · 88
- A HEAD FULL OF SPACE · 90
- WHEN EYES · 92
- PETUNIAS · 94
- IN MY ABSENCE · 94
- YOU SWEEP · 96
- NOW THAT WE ARE PARTING · 98
- GREENFIELD · 100

WIND SHEEN · 105
- THE FIRST NOTE · 106
- GULLS SHRIEK · 108
- WATERMELON SUN · 110
- SEA-BIRDS SCREECH · 112
- WIND TORN MINARET · 114
- CRACKS OF LIGHT · 116
- WHITE COLUMNS · 118
- SEA-COLOURED EYES · 120
- THE BLUE WOOL · 122
- A GRAIN OF WIND · 124
- SEA GRASS · 126
- WIND · 126
- PINES · 128

About the Author · 132
Translator's Postscript · 138

太陽の扉 ············· 75
　ふと出会った ············· 77
　声で判ったよ ············· 79
　赤いパン ············· 81
　水の中の目は ············· 81
　忍びよるのは ············· 83
　時は凍り ············· 85
　贈り物は ············· 87
　頬笑みは ············· 89
　空っぽの頭は ············· 91
　眼が雲の ············· 93
　ペチュニア ············· 95
　姿をかくして ············· 95
　あなたは掃き出す ············· 97
　今私達は別れるのだ ············· 99
　緑の野原は ············· 101

煌めく風 ············· 105
　蝉の ············· 107
　かもめが鳴く ············· 109
　西瓜の太陽が ············· 111
　海鳥たちが甲高く鳴く ············· 113
　風に引き裂かれたミナレットは ············· 115
　シャッターの隙間に ············· 117
　白い柱が ············· 119
　海色の眸が ············· 121
　青色の毛糸が ············· 123
　風が一粒 ············· 125
　海の草は ············· 127
　風は ············· 127
　松の木が ············· 129

　訳者紹介 ············· 136

詩集　煌めく風

2019年2月14日　第1刷発行
著　者　リジア・シュムクーテ
翻訳者　薬師川虹一
発行人　左子真由美
発行所　㈱竹林館
〒530-0044 大阪市北区東天満2-9-4 千代田ビル東館7階FG
Tel 06-4801-6111　Fax 06-4801-6112
郵便振替 00980-9-44593　URL http://www.chikurinkan.co.jp
印刷・製本　モリモト印刷株式会社
〒162-0813 東京都新宿区東五軒町3-19
Ⓒ Lidija Šimkutė
Ⓒ Kōichi Yakushigawa　2019 Printed in Japan
ISBN978-4-86000-400-2　C0098
定価はカバーに表示しています。落丁・乱丁はお取り替えいたします。

WIND SHEEN / poems

Lidija Šimkutė
Translation: Kōichi Yakushigawa
First published by CHIKURINKAN Jan. 2019
2-9-4-7FG, Higashitenma, Kita-ku, Osaka, Japan
http://www.chikurinkan.co.jp
Printed by MORIMORO PRINT CO.,Ltd. Tokyo, Japan
All rights reserved